Father Wore A Pink Vest

*The story of a young Rose-breasted Grosbeak
from the time it hatches until its fall migration*

Kathrine Snodgrass Flanagan

with Carolyn Flanagan Seierstad

Illustrating Artist Connie Freund Whiteside
Watercolor Artist Marilyn Kilpin Fuerstenberg

Published by Orange Hat Publishing 2021
ISBN 9781645382133

For information, please contact:
Orange Hat Publishing
www.orangehatpublishing.com
Waukesha, WI

CONTENTS

DEDICATION

This is my mother's book. She wrote this story with the hope that all who read it would come to know and love birds as she did. My mother loved family, teaching, birds, and children of all ages, sizes, shapes, and colors. But above all, she loved my father.

Although small in stature, his love for her was huge. He lifted her up, helped her to fly and to live her dreams throughout her 90 years of life. Two of her dreams were to teach and to spend time bird-watching, both of which she did with exuberance and joy. She loved sharing her bird-watching experiences and embellishing them with excitement, humor, and a bit of exaggeration.

I believe it would have been her wish to dedicate this book to the kind, loving, faithful, and humble man I called Dad.

-Carroll Edward Flanagan

FOREWORD

Madame. Madame Flanagan. Grande-Mere. The name evokes immense amounts of adoring memories for hundreds, if not thousands, of French students from the small world of Whitewater High School. Those memories could be her incredible enthusiasm in class, asking us to repeat, "Bonjour, Monsieur Thibaut," or perhaps it could be having us do weekly "resumes" of a filmstrip, or maybe it was the annual Mardi Gras festivals that would transform the entire high school cafeteria into a new, French-speaking land. Whatever it was, it was always creative, passionate, and full of "Madame love." Students and kids were her life, and she made sure that each and every one of them felt special and unique. I sure did. She changed my life.

In high school, Madame once showed me a children's book that she had written called *Father Wore a Pink Vest*. I was so enchanted by it that I decided to try to write it into a children's musical. Had I ever attempted to write a musical before? No. But, it was Madame, with her eternal wisdom and support, who said that I should go for it and gave me her blessing. Thus sparked the beginning of my career as a lifelong musical theatre composer/playwright and teacher.

Madame was special that way. She believed in you. She believed that you could do things that would make the world a better place. She did that in her teaching, and she did that in her writing. In her book, she wrote about simple truths of life's lessons lost, learned, and lived. I guess I always saw myself a bit like Bug - the runt, the one who was frightened, the one who maybe got into too much trouble, the one who was curious and adoring, and mostly, the one who was, and still is, in awe of this huge, wide world of ours. Maybe deep down inside, we all are a bit like Bug.

I can only hope that you will experience some of the simple wisdom and guidance of this book, and perhaps then, you might feel a morsel of the great soul of Madame Flanagan. For hers was a soul much too large to encapsulate in only one mere book and life. She was a tour-de-force that lives on through all those she touched, and I am forever grateful and humbled to have been a part of her life and legacy.

James Olm
Retired Chair of the Department of Theatre and Dance
Casper College

Author's Note ...

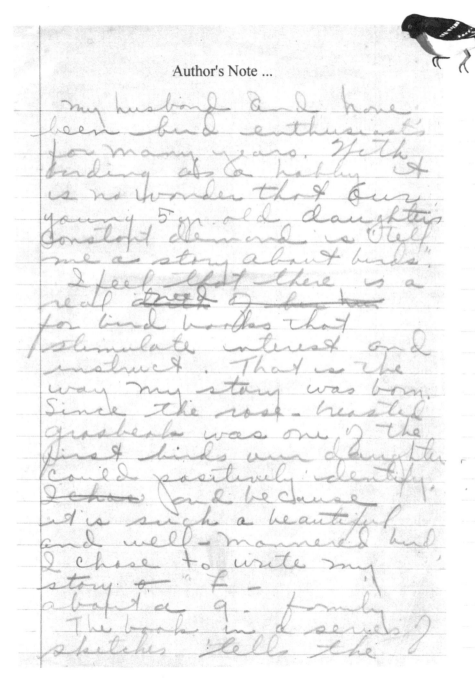

Kay Flanagan
Whitewater, Wisconsin
Summer, 1948

Kathrine's Notes

My husband and I have been bird enthusiasts for many years. With birding as a hobby it is no wonder that our young 5-year-old daughter's constant demand is "tell me a story about birds".

I feel that there is a real need for bird books that stimulate interest and instruct. That is the way my story was born.

Since the Rose-breasted Grosbeak was one of the first birds our daughter could positively identify and because it is such a beautiful and well-mannered bird I chose to write my story, Father Wore A Pink Vest, about a grosbeak family.

The book in a series of sketches tells the story of a grosbeak from the time it hatches until its fall migration.

Other bird characters and facts about birds in general appear in the story.

Kathrine Snodgrass Flanagan

1910-2001

CAROLYN'S NOTES

Father Wore A Pink Vest is my mother's story. Here is how it happened. It has been a part of my life as long as I can remember. Sometimes, she read me the story, written in pencil on old, soft lined paper, but mostly she told it to me from memory, always adding exciting characters, adventures, and new lessons in vivid detail. Although there was talk of publishing, it was never done.

Years passed without my thinking much about it, but the memory was always there, somewhere on a dusty bookshelf at the back of my mind, popping up from time to time. With the coming of the COVID-19 pandemic in 2020, that memory kept recurring. One day, I dug out the old manuscript and some old sketches by my cousin, Connie. I dusted them off, thought a lot about it and decided to give it a try.

Along with her original manuscript, I found Mom's roughly written notes about her thoughts as she wrote. I discovered that she wrote *Father Wore A Pink Vest* in 1948, when I was five years old. As others read the original story, I was encouraged to do some editing. They believed that, to hold the attention of today's children and to incorporate even more lessons, some changes were needed.

At first, I was very hesitant about changing Mom's story. Then Jim Olm, a former French student and dear friend of hers, told me that making some changes to this 72-year-old book was the best way to ensure people would pick it up, learn about birds, and pass it on, as was Mom's initial desire. After more discussion with Jim and others, I was convinced some work needed to be done. That's why there's a "With Carolyn Flanagan Seierstad" by her name.

My cousin, Connie, readily agreed to do more drawings, and my good friend and high-school classmate, Marilyn, agreed to watercolor paint them. With no idea of what we were getting into, the three of us took our first steps in building the book you now hold.

Carolyn Flanagan Seierstad
Janesville, Wisconsin
Summer, 2020

An Egg Is Hatched

Three miles west of the Big Marsh is the Beautiful Orchard of Farmer Littlefield. It was there, in the scrub oak standing next to the apple trees, that I first opened my eyes.

All at once, the dark, quiet place I was living in had become too small. Something stirring strangely inside of me made me push, peck, and wiggle hard. Suddenly there was a cracking noise. The eggshell broke from all around me, and I saw the world.

I was a baby Grosbeak!

I Meet Mother and Father

The first thing I heard was a sweet voice saying, "Father, see! The third spotted blue egg has finally hatched. The other two hatched days ago. What a puny thing he is ... all mouth and thin as a blade of grass."

I squinted up at a brown and tan striped figure that was bending over me. "I'm your Mother," she said. Then, pointing with her wing to another bird, she added. "Here is your Father."

By this time, I had yawned and stretched and managed to get my eyes open. They nearly popped out of my head! For there was the most beautiful creature I could imagine. His back, head and chin were black as night, and his wings were barred with white. His eyes were shiny and excited. However, it was something else that made me stare and gasp. For on his shirt, his snow white shirt, my father wore a pink vest.

5

We Are Named

"Now you must meet the rest of your family," said Mother. "You have a brother and sister." I turned around and stared beak to beak at two such homely, funny looking things that I laughed and laughed.

"Don't make fun of them, Son," said Mother, "because you look exactly like they do ... only more so." To find out I was so dreadful looking was more than I could stand, and I began to cry.

"No sniveling," said Father. "You are all fine babies, but you need a little time. After you get a bit of flesh on your bones and grow a few feathers, you'll look like real birds. Now for your names."

"I've always wanted a Rosie and Willie," said Mother.

"All right, although I've never cared for such fancy, newfangled names. Willie and Rosie you are," Father said, pointing a wing at my brother and sister. "But this one, I name," he insisted, touching me. "I'd like something old-fashioned and strong. I will call you 'Potato Bug.' Your grandfather and great-grandfather were both named 'Potato Bug.' They were both well-known and loved in the Beautiful Orchard. Because you're so small, we'll just call you 'Bug' for now."

So, Willie, Rosie, and Bug we were.

'Willie'   'Rosie'   'Bug'

Our First Lesson

"This is our home, and it's called a nest," said Mother. "Your father picked out this spot in the Beautiful Orchard when he was a young bird on his first migration. We've lived here ever since."

"I'm so proud of my beautiful home and family. Let's all help to keep this place clean," said Father. He spread his wings and flew around the tree singing happily.

"It's important for you to know this is always a safe place for you," said Mother. "Not all of our neighbors are kind. There are dangers in the Wide World that you don't yet know about. In time, you will learn where it is safe for us and where it's not."

We Eat And Grow

For ten days, we did nothing but eat, sleep, and grow. We never got filled up. Father and Mother took turns poking funny tasting things down our throats. He usually brought us the juiciest bugs. Mother said we were lucky because many Father birds don't help feed their babies. Often what he fed us tasted strange and really terrible, but he was always patient. "Just try a little at first, until you're used to it."

Our Family

One morning, Father perched above the nest and said, "It's time to learn about your family." Patting his pink vest, he said, "We are Rose-breasted Grosbeaks, part of a family called 'finches.' The finch family is larger than any other."

At this, Willie proudly puffed out his chest, but Father quickly responded, "Now don't feel too smart about it! All birds of all families have special things about them that shouldn't be compared or challenged. These are called traits. Never make fun of or laugh at family differences."

"As finches, we Grosbeaks have some rules we always try to stick by..."

1. Be helpful to farmers.

2. Be kind to other birds.

3. Keep your voice soft and melodious.

4. Don't eat too many cankerworms.

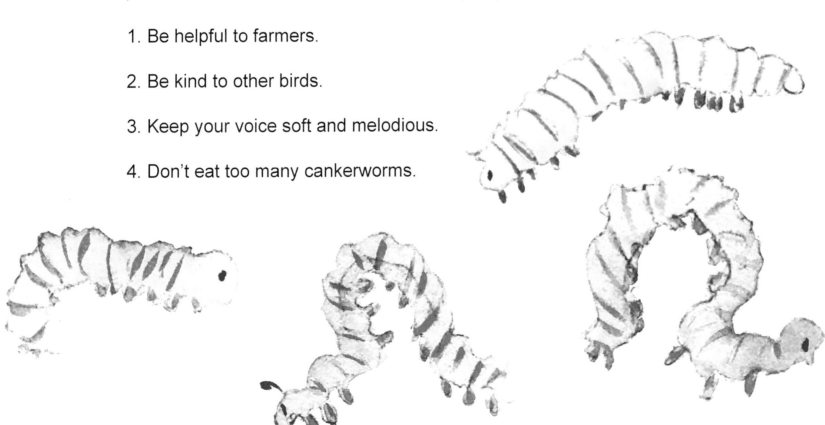

Learning to Fly

"The time has come," said Mother, pushing all three of us onto the branch, "for you to learn to fly. There's nothing to it. Remember, flap your wings to and fro, and away you go." Willie and Rosie squeaked happily.

I felt a little sick.

"First do your exercises.

Wings up.

Now, one, two,

up, down,

up, down

See, it's easy," said Mother, flying around the branch.

I felt worse.

"What's the matter, Bug?" asked Mother

"When I get my right wing up, the left one is down. When I get my left one up, the right one is down," I gulped. "And it's such an awfully long way to the ground." I closed my eyes tightly to hold back the tears.

13

"Just relax and try again," said Mother.

"One, two,

up, down,

up, down.

That's right, Willie and Rosie ... now faster. See, you're flying."

And they were!

They flipped and flopped around, but they were really flying! I was so em-barrassed, I crawled back into the nest. I'd never be able to fly.

I was too scared and miserable to try anymore.

14

In the meantime, Rosie and Willie were giggling
and flying happily around and around.

"What is it now, Bug?" said Mother as she kept trying to coax
me onto the branch.

"I can't,
          I can't!
                    I'll never fly!"

I screamed as she kept nudging and poking me, trying to
push me from the nest.

15

Just then, there was a whir of wings, and Father flew down. I was even more embarrassed! I wanted him to be proud of me, but there I was being nothing but a baby.

"Now, Bug, what's all this?" he asked. "What's the matter?"

"I can't fly!

I just can't!

The ground is so far away, and I'm afraid I'll fall."

"Don't look at the ground," said Father. "The ground is for people. We're birds, and the sky is ours. Look up and see how blue the sky is through the oak leaves.

That's where we'll go ...

you and I ...

up ...

up ...

gently up.

I'll go first."

Suddenly, I wasn't afraid. Father was right.
The sky was beautiful, and I wanted to get
up into it. Up and down my wings went ...
       slowly at first ...
but then faster and faster ...
       stronger and stronger ...

Rosie and Willie screamed, "Bug took off! Bug took off!

Look at him fly!"

"Father, Mother, I'm doing it! I can fly!" And off I went, following Father up and up into the beautiful blue sky.

19

Willie Learns A Lesson

"Mother! Father! Rosie! Bug! ... C-c-c-come q-q-q-quick! I saw a ... whoops," said Willie as he tumbled into a heap on the nest floor.

"Take it easy," said Mother. "No need to get so excited. Sit down, take a deep breath. Now, Willie, what did you see?"

"Oh, Mother, Father, g-get all the birds in the orchard. We must go to the Crested Flycatcher's nest. There is a snake in it! It'll eat the eggs!"

"Oh, Willie," smiled Father, "that wasn't a real snake. It was just a snake skin. Snakes shed their skin, and when they do, Mrs. Crested Flycatcher finds them and puts them in her nest to scare away enemies who would eat her eggs or hurt her babies."

"It is a scary sight, and I can see how you'd be worried. We birds need to watch out for each other, and your idea to help Mrs. Crested Flycatcher was a good one. You've just shown us a good example of one of those rules we learned about ... Be kind to other birds ... and you've made me proud."

The next morning, Father flew to the nest and was shocked. "What in the Wide World is this, and who did it?" he exclaimed.

"I did," said Willie, proudly sticking out his chest. "It's a snake skin I found and I brought it to protect our nest. I'm sure if it keeps the Crested Flycatcher's nest safe, it'll do the same for ours."

"Oh no, Willie, please take it away," said Mother, shuddering. "Snake skins are not for Grosbeaks."

When I thought it over at bedtime, I thought Willie had been really smart.

The Purple Martins

One morning, Willie, Rosie, and I came flying to the nest like a swarm of bees ... swirling, dipping, diving, and suddenly dropping, breathless onto the floor. "Mother, Mother," said Rosie, breathing heavily. "The Purple Martins' house is the worst mess in the neighborhood. There is chaff and leaves, and grass and feathers, and other smelly stuff coming out of all the holes and piling up on the ground underneath. It's disgusting!"

Mother turned slowly, adjusted her apron, and told the fledglings to sit and settle down. "I've never heard you talk like that," she said, frowning. "I'm disappointed in you, and I think it's time we talked about the problems birds have in trying to find a safe, warm home."

"I was starting to make lunch, but this is important," she said with a stern voice. "You don't know what others go through and how lucky we are that Father found this perfect place for our nest."

"I was just talking to Mrs. Purple Martin this morning. She and her relatives just arrived from their spring migration. They had rented the big Martin House from Farmer Wheatgrower for this season and expected it would be a nice, warm, safe place. But, what did they find?"

"The house was filled with dirt and litter left by English Sparrows last winter. The Purple Martins were very tired after their long flight, but they did their best to get some cleaning done before falling asleep. Then water dripped on them all night from a leak in the roof. I've never seen such a mess!"

"People who put up birdhouses should keep them clean and repaired. However, many don't. They just want the enjoyment of seeing beautiful birds in their yards and hearing their sweet voices tweeting and chirping happily throughout the day."

24

Willie, Rosie, and I hung our heads, feeling awful for our quick and unthinking judgment of the Martins. We had no idea! We told Mother we were sorry and agreed that we had learned another important lesson. We didn't tell her how we had teased and laughed at the little Martins.

"Tonight after our potato bug pancakes, I plan to go over and help the Martins clean. They are some of the nicest, most friendly birds here, and it's a shame how they've been treated."

Mother was always helping other birds, and we were very proud of her. But, it wasn't only her kindness that made us so happy. Father was to take care of us! We were wild with excitement. We always had a great time with Father, especially when he sang us stories.

After the last potato bug was poked neatly down our throats, Mother tied her brown scarf around her head. "Now, Father," she reminded him, "put the children to bed early this time. When the first star peeks through the lone elm tree, they are to go to bed ... no later."

"Let's get Father's back to the lone elm tree, so he can't see the sky and tell what time it is," said Willie, who was always full of ideas.

A Night With Father

Taking a sunflower seed from his bill, Father smoothed his feathers, patted his pink vest, and began to sing. Most birds are quiet when it's dark, but Father was always bubbling with song. His music came from deep inside. We tried not to be too proud, but we thought he was the most wonderful singer in the Beautiful Orchard, or the Big Meadow, or even in the Wide World.

Lying snug in our pajamas and looking up at the starry sky, we listened to Father. He sang of his first taste of potato bug, the building of our oak tree nest, and the three eggs that hatched.

Then he told us of getting ready for the Big Migration, and of flying through the dark of night with the wind in his face, and of the time at the Big Marsh when the Red-tailed Hawk nearly pulled out his tail feathers. On and on he sang, until the stars grew bright and our heads nodded. It seemed as if his warbling and bubbling notes came from the round, golden moon that rose high over the Beautiful Orchard. Surely there was no one more wonderful than Father, we thought as our eyes closed.

Father's Song

Sleep my little Grosbeaks three
Safe in your nest in the green oak tree
Fold your wings, and sleep each one
Until the rising of the sun.

29

"Oh my, the children are sleepy this morning," said Mother. "I had to peck their heads three times to wake them up. And what is wrong with you?" She asked Father, who was gargling with elderberry juice.

"I seem to have lost my voice," croaked Father, lowering his eyes and looking a little guilty. "It has been a wet spring. Maybe I caught a slight cold."

30

Bug's Scary Adventure

One cool and rainy day, Willie, Rosie, and I flew into Farmer Littlefield's big red barn to stay dry. In the barn, very big black and white creatures looked up at us from their strange-looking cages. They had huge, sad eyes and made the most outrageous noises.

31

We played "Hide and Find" and raced each other from one end of the barn to the other. When we flew too close to the ground, orange cats jumped up and tried to catch us.

I was having a delightful time
soaring just beneath the ceiling,
swirling, climbing, diving, and gliding
around and around. I didn't notice
when Willie and Rosie chased a
butterfly out into the rain.

It was wonderful, but then I got out
of breath, became dizzy, and I felt
a little sick. When I flew to the great
door, it was closed!

I was scared and shaking and felt
even more sick.

I sat on a big piece of dried yellow grass with a string
tied around it, trying to catch my breath and settle my
stomach. The yellow cats crept toward me with their tails
swishing and their big eyes glowing. I could barely stand.

Then I saw the sky through a hole way up high near
where I'd been flying. I'd found a way out!

I headed for it fast ...

as fast as I could go.

33

Closer ...

closer ...

I could make it, then ...

BANG!

Everything was black ... no ceiling ... no hole ... no sky!

I was on my back with my beak aching and my head feeling like it was cracked open.

Then I fell asleep.

The next thing I knew, I was floating up toward the face of a little person wearing short pants. "Oh, you poor little thing. Look at what's happened to you," she said. "Don't worry, you'll be alright. I will carry you outside where it's cool and shady and put you under your nest."

I was gently placed on the grass, and the little person stepped back. I struggled to stand on my shaky legs and then flew up to my family with an exciting story to tell and probably a new lesson to learn.

The Singing Lesson

Willie, Rosie, and I were perched on a big limb. Father was giving us our first singing lesson. It was exciting to think that someday we'd be able to warble like him.

"Try it again," said Father to Willie and me as his rich, full voice drifted through the orchard. Willie and I threw our heads back and tried as hard as we could. I thought we sounded pretty good for the first lesson, although Willie squeaked on some of the high notes.

"You're learning fast," said Father, looking pleased, "but now let's listen to you, Rosie. Most girl birds don't sing, but we Grosbeaks do," said Father proudly, patting his vest.

"Now sing, Rosie."

"Mmm - mmm - mm," struggled Rosie, barely making a sound.

"What's wrong with you, Rosie? Open your beak and sing!"

"I can't," squirmed Rosie, trying to hide her head under her wing.

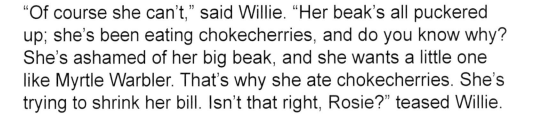

"Of course she can't," said Willie. "Her beak's all puckered up; she's been eating chokecherries, and do you know why? She's ashamed of her big beak, and she wants a little one like Myrtle Warbler. That's why she ate chokecherries. She's trying to shrink her bill. Isn't that right, Rosie?" teased Willie.

Rosie hung her head.

"*Yeth*," she managed to say.

I thought Rosie needed someone to stick up for her, so I told Father the story.

"Yesterday, when we were laughing and making fun of the Martins' messy house, one of the young Martins flew fast right at us. I was afraid he'd fly right into me and send me falling from the sky.

Ha Ha Ha

Oooh

Ha Ha Ha

'We can clean our house to be just as good as yours," the little Martin yelled, "but you can't do anything at all to change those gross, ugly beaks of yours!'

That's when we all flew home to tell Mother, and then she scolded us and told us about what had happened to the Purple Martins, and then we were sorry."

I took a big breath and sat down.

Father looked at the three of us, as we again hung our heads over our big mistake. "What you did to the little Purple Martin is called 'bullying,' and it is something we Rose-breasted Grosbeaks do not allow in our families. I know you feel badly about your treatment of the Martins," he said, "and I believe you've learned a valuable lesson that you won't soon forget."

His eyes twinkled as he flew to Rosie and spread his wings around her. "My dear girl," he said with love and understanding in his voice. "My silly little girl, to envy something another bird has ... I don't blame you for thinking Myrtle's little beak is pretty. She's such a tiny bird, she'd look funny with a big one. But we are given certain features to help us. Mother is dressed in brown and tan to protect her on the nest. Myrtle lives on insects and needs a needle-like beak to catch them. The Nighthawk has whiskers around his beak that spread out like a net to catch mosquitoes as he flies.

We are mostly seed-eaters. In fact, our beaks are so special and important, we are named after them. Rose-breasted Grosbeaks. *Gros* means *big* ... big beak ... Grosbeaks. Think how handy your beak is in cracking open sunflower seeds. Myrtle couldn't do that. She probably couldn't even pick up a sunflower seed."

"I love thunflower theeds," said Rosie.

"Of course you do, and you could never eat them if it weren't for your beak. So cheer up and be happy that you are well and strong just the way you are," said Father.

"I will be ... Really, I will be," said Rosie eagerly.

43

The Wrens

One morning, Willie, who had been visiting the neighborhood, flew up saying, "Father, Father, I was just playing with the little Wrens and gee, they're covered with lice! The little Purple Martin says the Wrens are 'lousy,' and the little Robin said so, too."

"Willie, there are some words Grosbeaks don't use ... and especially not to describe another bird. Lousy is one of those words, and I do not want you using it to describe Wrens or anyone else."

"But, Father, they really are," insisted Willie.

"They're covered with lice ... I mean ... they are ... they are ... covered," finished Willie weakly, catching Father's eye. "Well, what should I call it, then?"

"You don't need to call it anything," said Father. "Just don't talk about it. I hope you didn't tease the Wrens or bully them."

"I think we already had this lesson, only it was about the Purple Martins," said Mother, who had just flown in. "Don't blame the Wrens. It's the fault of the people who keep Wren houses. Many baby Wrens die each year from mites and lice that live in Wren houses all winter long ... even through ice and snow."

"I can't help it! I still say the young Wrens are full of li—I mean, *you-know-what*," said Willie, avoiding Mother's stern look.

"Let's remember all the lessons you've learned, *especially* to never bully other birds. Now let's talk about the Big Migration," said Mother, quickly changing the subject.

A Sad Lesson

Pip Pip

One morning, Father was gone a long time. He didn't sing his happy homecoming song when he did arrive. Instead we heard,

Pip Pip

the squeaky warning call of Grosbeaks. When he flew down to the nest, he looked sad and tired.

"How about a nice piece of tent worm pie?" said Mother.

Father's shoulders hung and his eyes were sad. "Today I saw Mr. Mourning Dove die. He had just left his wife and babies to seek tender worms for their lunch. While he was looking around, a little Crosspatch in trousers sneaked up and

BANG!

Mr. Mourning Dove was dead!"

"Sadly, the little Crosspatch has never been taught not to shoot birds. Lately, he's been shooting at everything in sight. Last week, he shot three rabbits and carried them away. This time at least he seemed to be sad about taking a life ... or maybe that's just because Farmer Crosspatch finally took his shooting stick away.

I chose the oak in Farmer Littlefield's orchard for our nest because he and his family love birds and are kind to us. But Farmer Crosspatch is a very different story. Let's hope that will all change because of this terrible thing."

"Yes," we all agreed.

"Now, you fledglings must learn about 'People.'" Father put his glasses over his sharp, black eyes, went to the twig bookcase, and picked up a big book. "'Book of People East of the Rockies,'" he read as he turned the page.

"People are creatures who walk on the earth and live in very big houses. Like birds, they come in many different colors, shapes, and sizes. All of them are much larger than birds and have traits that help them survive. In spite of different colors, shapes, and sizes, people are all alike.

But, you need to learn one big difference. Some love birds and others do not. Some love to watch and listen to birds; they even make long lists of the different species they see each year. These people do whatever they can to make our lives better and even provide safe bird houses and food."

"People who do not love birds often find them a nuisance and are annoyed by them. We try to stay far away from them. Today I want you to learn that some people, like Farmer Crosspatch and his son, are a danger to us.

Sometimes they climb trees, steal our eggs, and hurt baby birds. Today I saw one kill Mr. Mourning Dove. Although it's important to never forget people can be dangerous and to use our instincts to sense danger, it's also important to give them a chance. We cannot live in fear. Instead, fly up into the Great Blue Sky and be grateful for the beauty in the world all around you."

Father closed the book.

Migration Day

This morning, when I opened my eyes, I thought at first it was just another bright September day. Then I began to feel a strange tickling inside of me ... a tickling that whispered, "Bug, Bug, this is it." I flew with Rosie and Willie to the sunflower patch where many birds were gathered. They had been dull and quiet for several weeks, but today they were excited, and everyone was chirping at once.

"Father, is this ...?"

"Yes, Son, this is the day."

"When do we leave? Where do we go?"

"Sometime tonight we'll fly to Central America."

"Where's that?" asked Rosie.

"It's very far, and we take many nights to fly there. Sometimes it will be cold, and you will see snow along the way," smiled Father, "but it's beautiful and warm in Central America, and we'll find plenty to eat all winter. Now our bodies are fat, and our wings are strong for the flight. You'd know how to get there even if I didn't show you. That's born inside of you because you're a Grosbeak."

"It's called 'Instinct.'"

All day long, we ate and watched birds gathering for the Big Flight. When the sun began to sink behind the Beautiful Orchard and the stars peeked through the Big Heavens, Father called us all together.

Mother, Father, Willie, Rosie, and I were perched on Farmer Littlefield's fence.

The orchard buzzed with the excited chirping of birds.

Rosie squeezed my wing.

"Soon we'll be off, Bug," she whispered.

Then suddenly, as if a great wind had picked us up in its mighty arms, we rose in a flock,

up into the dark blue night with its smattering of stars.

Up,

up,

into the cool fragrance of the September air, we soared and started on our long trip to a faraway, unknown land.

This is wonderful, I thought as I flew along with my family and hundreds of bird relatives. *This really is wonderful! This is the reason I was hatched and fed and carefully taught by Mother and Father.*

Flying out into the Big Wide World made me feel warm inside, and good.

61

Then, as we flew over great cities shining in the night and over great mountains, quiet and dark, I thought of Father and all he taught me. And I said to myself, "Someday, when I have fledglings of my own, I'll try to be just like Father ... Best of all, next year and in other years to come, I too will wear upon my shirt a **bright pink vest**."

62

The Rose-breasted Grosbeak

God painted our backs from the night itself,
Our breasts from the Northern snows.
He gave us a bill like an ice cream cone,
Then tinted our breast with a rose.

He gave us a bubbling, lovely song,
That we warble from morn till night.
And two white-splashed wings that are firm and strong,
To carry us far in flight.

The mother He dressed in brown and tan,
And drew a line over her eye.
In safety she watches her babes in the nest,
And teaches them how to fly.

Oh, happy is he who knows these birds,
And watches them go by,
They add beauty and song to a dreary day,
They're the loveliest things in the sky.

-Kay Flanagan

ACKNOWLEDGMENTS

When making the decision to get Mom's book published, I never expected to become its editor. I'm deeply grateful to all those who helped to get it published!

I appreciate Orange Hat Publishing for their support and assistance from the time they first accepted *Father Wore a Pink Vest*. Many thanks to Kaeley Dunteman for her patience and expert help in editing, cover design, suggestions, and in making what at times seemed endless changes and corrections. You've been a delight to work with!

My dear cousin, Connie Whiteside, shared her amazing talent through her imaginative drawings. She was patient and always willing to make changes when necessary. Her wonderful sense of humor, faith in our ultimate goal, and prayers when things got rough helped ground us and keep things in perspective. Thank you, Precious Lamb!

My good friend, Marilyn Fuerstenberg, was dedicated to making this book educational, consistent, and attractive to children. She expertly painted Connie's drawings, always striving to make them 'just so.' She spent many hours matching and laying out the completed pictures and text with endless patience. Her ideas for many of the pictures brought light and life to the story. Of all the work put into this book, she did the most! Words alone cannot express my deep and sincere gratitude for all you've done and mostly for your lasting friendship!

Merci beaucoup to Jim Olm who contributed ideas, listened, encouraged me to make changes and wrote a beautiful tribute to Mom in his Foreward.

Thank you to Jim Whiteside, Connie's husband, who was wonderfully prompt in getting her drawings to us, always adding humorous little messages that made us smile.

Thank you to my sister-in-law, Alberta Seierstad, who volunteered to proofread the manuscript, and did so precisely and accurately, always taking the time to provide welcome words of support.

Thank you to Hailey Fuerstenberg, Marilyn's 10-year-old great-granddaughter, who agreed to be an early reader, giving us a better perspective of how the completed book would come across to children her age.

My deep and constant thanks go to my husband, Don Seierstad, who read the story and shared his ideas. As he always is, Don was patient and supportive, always reminding me of our goal, always being there for me when I needed him.

Finally and mostly, I am forever grateful to my Mom and Dad. Together, they shared their love of birds with me, teaching me to identify a great number of species. That gift remains with me today as I see and hear the beautiful little reminders of their presence tweeting, singing, and warbling all around me each day.

1. Rose-breasted Grosbeak   2. English Sparrow   3. Red-tailed Hawk   4. Mourning Dove   5. Myrtle Warbler
6. House Wren   7. Robin   8. Crested Flycatcher   9. Purple Martin   10. Nighthawk

CPSIA information can be obtained
at www.ICGtesting.com
Printed in the USA
LVRC060452010421
683143LV00001B/1